The Adventures of Lady Eleanor

A Very Very Naughty Tale

Elizebeth Moody

ELIZABETH MOODY

The Adventures of Lady Eleanor

A Very Very Naughty Tale

First published by Julia Cammack 2024

Copyright © 2024 by Elizabeth Moody

All rights reserved. No part of this publication may be reproduced, stored or transmitted in any form or by any means, electronic, mechanical, photocopying, recording, scanning, or otherwise without written permission from the publisher. It is illegal to copy this book, post it to a website, or distribute it by any other means without permission.

This novel is entirely a work of fiction. The names, characters and incidents portrayed in it are the work of the author's imagination. Any resemblance to actual persons, living or dead, events or localities is entirely coincidental.

Elizabeth Moody asserts the moral right to be identified as the author of this work.

Elizabeth Moody has no responsibility for the persistence or accuracy of URLs for external or third-party Internet Websites referred to in this publication and does not guarantee that any content on such Websites is, or will remain, accurate or appropriate.

Designations used by companies to distinguish their products are often claimed as trademarks. All brand names and product names used in this book and on its cover are trade names, service marks, trademarks and registered trademarks of their respective owners. The publishers and the book are not associated with any product or vendor mentioned in this book. None of the companies referenced within the book have endorsed the book.

First edition

This book was professionally typeset on Reedsy.
Find out more at reedsy.com

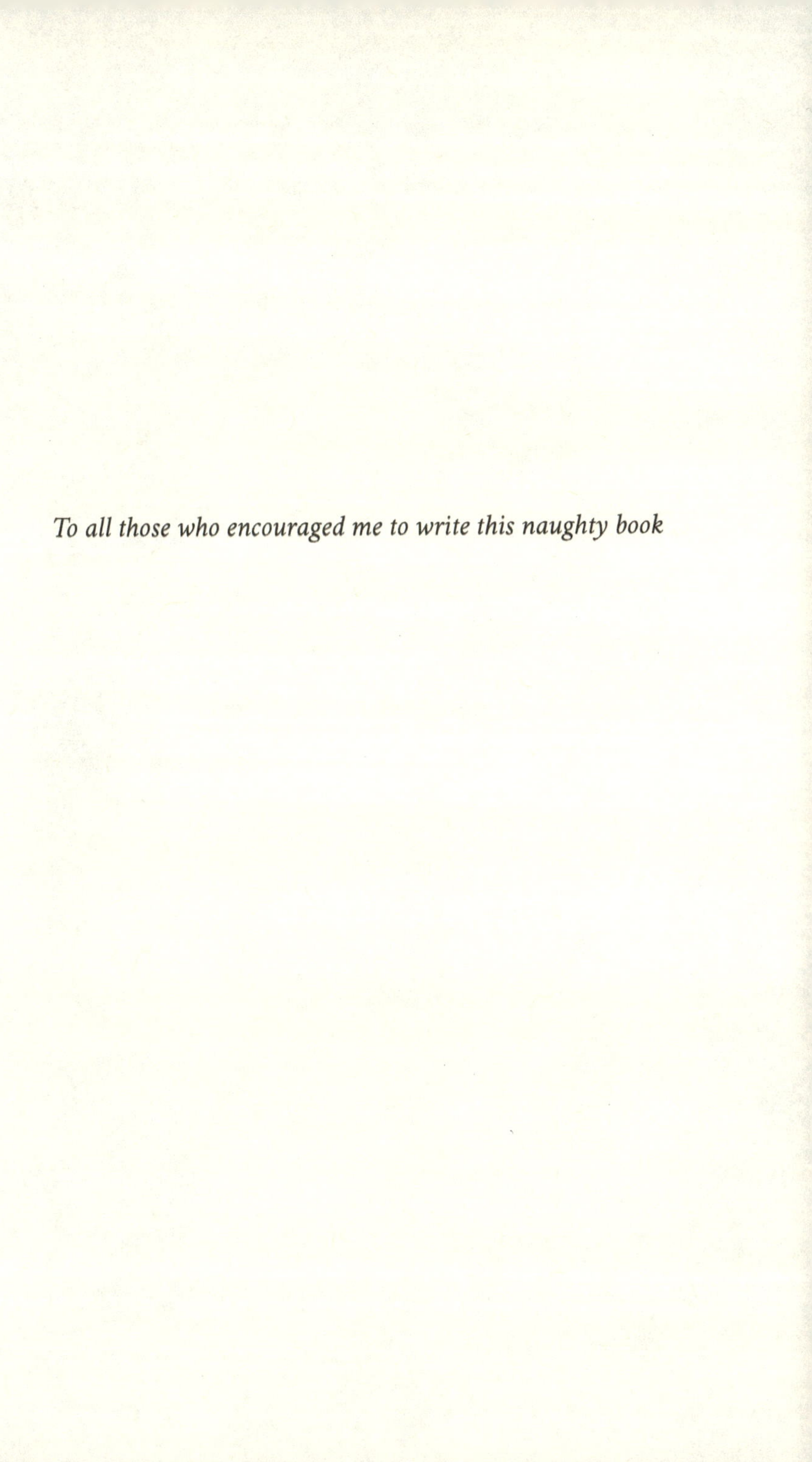

To all those who encouraged me to write this naughty book

Contents

Preface

There is no such thing as a moral or immoral book. A book should please the reader. If it does not, then the author has failed.

Acknowledgments

For friends that encouraged, critiqued and laughed about this book, and the wonderful Adam Hay who created the beautiful cover.

Introduction

Life is a series of learned lessons. What you do with them is your choice. Lady Eleanor made the choice to live life to the fullest at a time when women had little control over their lives.

I

Part One

Learning a Lesson

One

Chapter 1

A Trip Down the Stairs.

Eleanor was coming up on her 15th. birthday. Her father called her the runt of the litter and other unflattering things. The last of seven daughters, her mother had almost died birthing her and never missed an opportunity to remind her of that fact or tell her how ugly she was. Her sisters were beautiful and slim, with blond wavy hair, while hers was frizzy and a burnt red-brown mess that was uncontrollable. The one person in her life who had shown her kindness was her great aunt, her grandfather's stepdaughter, who had passed away last year.

Through hard work, their grandfather managed to accumulate property, upon which he raised sheep and grew crops. He had married a widow with one child, money, and land that he happily joined to his. He built a large manor house and was given a court appointment as governor and tax collector for the crown. Eleanor's father, his only son, inherited everything upon his death.

Her father found hard work and thrift unbecoming for a man of his standing. Instead, he preferred hunting, drinking, and only hobnobbing with persons he considered his equal. With no thought for the future, money flowed like wine. Soon, creditors began to appear at his door. His answer to this was to sell off land, or when each of his daughters became of marrying age, he doled out parcels of land as their dowry. There was little left when Eleanor came of marriageable age. Without a dowry, she would have little chance of a good marriage and besides, she was needed at home to care for her mother.

As long as her great aunt was alive, there had been some respite from her mother's tirades, but now they were non-stop. Not just the harsh words hurled at her but pinches and slaps when she was close enough to receive them. Eleanor would feed her mother and clean up the mess when her mother soiled the bed, insisting she couldn't reach the night jar soon enough. Eleanor's only purpose in life seemed to be caring for her parent. The fast-rushing river was an interesting alternative when she thought of the many years that lay ahead for her trapped in this misery.

Eleanor slept in an anti-room next to her mother's bedroom so she could be nearby if her mother needed anything. One night, when her mother was having trouble sleeping, she ordered Eleanor to fetch her some hot milk. Slipping on a robe, Eleanor went down to the kitchen, where the stove had been banked for the night. It took a minute to wake up the fire. She placed the pot on the flame and took down a cup. She was stirring the hot milk when she heard the scream. Pulling the pot off the fire, she rushed into the hall.

Her mother had become impatient while waiting for Eleanor to return, so she had come down intending to berate her daughter for being so slow. In her hast to descend the stairs, she missed a step, plunging forwards, and landed in a twisted heap on the cold marble floor below.

Eleanor stood transfixed, staring down at her mother's body. She had often thought of pushing her mother down these same stairs, but now, seeing her there, her head on a strange angle, the blood slowly dripping from her lips, Eleanor felt nothing. It all seemed surreal.

Two

Chapter 2

A Sad Arrangement and a New Discovery

Her mother had been buried in the family graveyard. The families had come and gone. The sisters shed the appropriate tears and departed as soon as possible. Her father stayed drunk for a week and then took up with the housekeeper. Eleanor couldn't be sure, but she felt they had been intimate long before her mother's death. She had come upon them several times in the hallways, whispering with each other. Now, their relationship was out in the open.

Lack of money had reduced the staff considerably. The housekeeper lorded it over the few that were left. Eleanor, too, was put to work cleaning and helping in the kitchen. She was more of a scullery maid than the daughter of the manor. Her bed had been placed in a tiny attic room after her father began sleeping with his new lady in her mother's bed. The blessing was that no one seemed to know or care what she did when her work was finished.

After everyone had gone to bed, if she wasn't too exhausted, she would slip out and swim in the river. The cold water gliding over her gave her a most pleasing thrill. Her nipples stiffened, and her whole body tingled. Her breasts were unfashionably full and round, not small and flat like her sisters. Eleanor had bound them to make them appear flat, but her sisters noticed and would make fun of her, calling her a sow.

One night, as Eleanor wrapped herself in her robe after her swim, the warmth of it only heightened the sensual feeling that coursed through her body. She began drying herself slowly, her breasts, then her legs. As she dried between her legs, the feeling became intense. Eleanor fell to the ground and continued rubbing herself, faster and faster, until her whole body exploded with pleasure.

It took her a while to return to normal. She didn't understand what had happened, but it was incredible. No one had ever spoken of this thing she had just experienced. Sleepy and happy, she returned to her room and slept soundly until daylight.

The next morning, she had her ears boxed by the housekeeper for daydreaming while scrubbing the pots, but nothing could ruin her day. As soon as she could, Eleanor escaped to her room. By the time the household was asleep, a sudden storm had spoiled all hope of taking a swim.

Lying in her bed and thinking of the night before, she felt the same need rising. Pulling up her nightdress, she put her hand between her legs and began slowly moving her fingers over the lips of her vagina. Once again, the sensation was incredible. She waited for the explosion, wanting it yet slowing the experience, enjoying the feeling as it rose to a climax.

After her breathing returned to normal, her vagina still begged for attention. Eleanor began the process once more, and this time, she tried putting her fingers inside while massaging the lips. The feeling was even more intense. Was this what it felt like to have a man inside you? She had been told it was a wife's duty to submit to their husband, but not once had they told her about the pleasure of being bedded.

Three

Chapter 3

A Change of Station

Months later, Eleanor found herself wedded. This odd change of events had come about because of a large debt. Her father had gambled at cards and lost as he usually did. He now owed so much money to a neighboring widower that he had offered his remaining daughter as payment.

Considering Eleanor's age and Lord Edwards's need for an heir, the childless widower was happy to oblige. Eleanor should have been unhappy with the arrangement, as her new husband was so much older, but instead of resenting the deal, she chose to appreciate it.

She had been nothing but a servant in her father's house, criticized and bullied by her father's lover. Now, she had a title, servants of her own, a husband who was kind to her, and an allowance to be spent as she saw fit. All she must do was to keep her husband happy. The critical place was in the bedroom. That was the challenge.

The problem was her husband's age. Eleanor had expectations of her first real sexual experience with a man. The thrill she had discovered alone would be even better with a partner. A young man, once aroused, would be firm and hard, but her poor husband was rather soft and flabby. Even if he managed to enter her vagina, his thrusting caused little reaction on Eleanor's part, and he was finished too soon. It left both of them frustrated.

One night as Eleanor tried to help him, she encircled his penis with her fingers. The tight fit excited him so much more than his previous attempts. He never realized he wasn't completely inside. Her husband was delighted with what he assumed had been his best performance in the bedroom in years. Eleanor saw no reason to enlighten him. An expensive gift lay on her pillow the next night. She would need to learn more about this sex thing. There appeared to be power in what you could accomplish in the bedroom.

Four

Chapter 4

M ary Clair.

Mary Clair had been married at a younger age than most. Her husband saw the need for patience with his new bride and, rather than frighten his young wife, had taken his time to consummate the marriage. The arranged marriage became a love match.

The one sadness for Mary Clair and her husband was their lack of children. Each pregnancy had ended in a miscarriage or stillbirth. People around them were blessed with more children than they wanted, but their nursery remained empty.

When it became clear there would be no heir to inherit the fortune or property when he died, Mary Clair's husband made an important decision. He was a magistrate in the provincial court, and as such, he had seen all that could befall women when their spouses died. The estate would pass to the closest male relative. That meant that the widow was at the mercy of the recipient. Too often, they were treated poorly or sent to a convent or poor house to live out their lives in despair. Rather than give all he had worked for to some distant, unknown male, he intended to take care of his wife.

As the years passed, he carefully and quietly sold everything to Mary Clair. Legal documents proved she was the rightful owner of the house, all the land it sat on, and any monies associated with the estate. No one could tell her what to do. She was a rich woman in her own right, and she would be left in complete control of everything following her husband's death.

Upon receiving the news of her brother's unexpected marriage, Mary Clair set out immediately to assess the situation for herself. He may have acquired a title with their father's death, but he was still her brother. Moreover, she had been told the new wife was much younger than Lord Edward and didn't have a dowry. Why would her brother make such a mistake in judgment? Had he developed dementia?

Five

Chapter 5

A New Friend and an Unknown Stranger

Lord Edward's sister, Mary Clair, was several years younger than her brother and had come to visit. She was there to have a good look at the new wife. To her surprise, her brother looked healthier and happier than he had in years. She had come to criticize this strange and unexpected marriage, assuming Eleanor was in it for the money and title. Instead, she found Eleanor a pleasant companion and a devoted wife, and devoid of avarice. The two were soon chatting away like old friends.

Lord Edward was giving a large party to introduce his new wife and to celebrate his sister's visit. Eleanor was glad to have her sister-in-law's help in planning the evening. She couldn't remember there ever being such an affair at her father's house. He would rather spend his money when he had some, in a pub with his friends. Mary Clair was very familiar with how to do such things as she and her late husband had been socially prominent and entertained often. Not only did she take charge, but she explained everything she did to Eleanor as she went.

There were guests to be counted, invitations to be printed, menus to consider, extra servants to interview and hire, as well as musicians to be brought in for the evening, to say nothing of the house that must be cleaned from top to bottom. Eleanor found the whole thing overwhelming. Thank God she didn't have to do it alone. Her sister-in-law was an unexpected blessing. She would owe it all to Mary Clair if the party were a success.

The night of the celebration, the house was filled with guests. Everyone appeared to be having a good time. Lady Eleanor had been introduced to so many people whose names she would never remember and smiled until her face ached. She had been unable to eat anything because her stomach was tied in knots. Mary Clair had stayed by her side for most of the evening, and Eleanor's husband was beaming with pride. Exhausted, all Eleanor wanted was to sit somewhere quiet and rest a minute away from the crowd.

The library appeared empty. Eleanor slipped into an oversize wing back chair and removed her shoes. Her head had begun to ache, and her corset was too tight. The evening had been everything her husband had wanted it to be, but now Eleanor just wanted all these people to leave.

A male voice made her nearly jump out of her skin. The gentleman apologized for startling her. He had been admiring the collection of fine books on the shelves and hadn't expected company. Coming forward to introduce himself, he bent to kiss her hand. It was as if she had been stung.

For a moment, she was unable to speak. When she finally found her voice, she stammered something about needing to join her husband.

Laughing, he said, "Perhaps you should put your shoes on first." He knelt and slipped a shoe on her naked foot. Eleanor stood up so fast she almost fell. He reached out to steady her. The touch of his fingers, first on her foot, and then on her arm had taken her breath away. Seizing her other shoe, Eleanor fled from the room.

Mary Clair found Eleanor leaning against the wall, her shoe clutched to her breast, as she attempted to steady her breathing. Her sister-in-law sat her down and brought her a brandy. Eleanor knew instinctively that it wouldn't be wise to explain precisely what had happened to her in the library.

People were beginning to leave. Putting on her other shoe, Eleanor joined her husband at the door to bid their guests goodnight. When, at last, everyone had gone, Edward couldn't wait to escort his wife to bed. The amount he had drank caught up to him as soon as his head hit the pillow, and he was fast asleep and snoring before Eleanor had undressed. She found sleep much harder to come by, and when at last she dozed off, her dreams were full of strange hands caressing her foot.

Six

Chapter 6

A Visitor.

Her sister-in-law had returned to her home after wishing the couple well and hinting about the significant gift she would bestow upon a niece or nephew. Eleanor assured her that was possible while doubting it herself.

Eleanor was learning things about the bedroom. If she undressed slowly in front of her husband and spent time caressing him, he was able to have a harder erection. He didn't last any longer, but he could penetrate her vagina before releasing his sperm. Perhaps she could give him the heir he so wanted. What a wonderful surprise that would be for her husband. She had become quite fond of this man.

After the death of his first wife, Lord Edward had let the estate's gardens go. Now, he was happy to engage gardeners to please his new wife. Eleanor delighted in watching the sadly overgrown roses bloom as a reward for the attention. Pathways had been cleared, and the broken fountain repaired. The hedges had been trimmed, and a kitchen garden now supplied them with fresh vegetables.

Eleanor had been happily inspecting everything. The long walk around the garden in the late afternoon sun was pleasant but hot. Feeling like a child again, she slipped off her shoes, hiked up her skirt, and sat on the fountain's edge dangling her feet in the cool water.

"Why is it that you find it impossible to keep your shoes on?"

Jumping up, dropping the edge of her skirt in the water in her hast, Eleanor turned to confront the speaker. Laughing, he reached in, seized her around the waist, and lifted her out of the fountain. Her first thought was to strike him. How could he be so bold? He reached down and picked up her shoes.

"May I help you? You will find the gravel path painful."

Eleanor seized her shoes and put them on. "How dare you take such liberties. What are you doing here?"

" I came to pay my respects to Lord Edward's new wife. He told me I would find you in the garden."

"You have a strange habit of sneaking up on people."

He laughed again. "Perhaps I should be belled like a cat."

Eleanor tried not to laugh, but the thought was so absurd she couldn't help it.

" Perhaps you should. You seem to know who I am, but we have never been introduced, sir."

He took her hand, bowed, and kissed it. Eleanor found it hard to breathe. Her face flushed, and she had no idea what he had said, so his name remained a mystery. Eleanor dared not look at him. She wanted to run away as fast as she could but forced herself to turn and walk slowly back to the house.

Lord Edward was waiting for them in the drawing room. He explained that Harold was the son of an old friend. Both he and his father had been among the guests at the party. Had they not met?

Harold answered for them both, saying he had not had the pleasure. When her husband invited him to stay for supper, Eleanor excused herself and fled from the room. Her heart was beating so hard she could hear it. Why was she being so foolish? Straightening her back, she marched to the kitchen to tell the cook that there would be an unexpected guest for dinner.

Harold spent the meal regaling them with tales of his travels. After supper, the men retired to the library for cigars and cognac. Eleanor sat in the drawing room, trying to read her book. Her mind kept repeating the scene in the garden. What was it about this man that had such an effect on her? Thinking about him caused her body to react. Her breasts ached, and moisture gathered between her legs. All she wanted was to retire to her bedroom and pleasure herself.

Harold bid them goodnight at last. Her husband was in fine spirits and followed her up the stairs. He was astonished at her aggression in the bedroom. She couldn't wait to remove her clothes, and soon, she was rubbing him and fondling his balls until he was ready. In a surprise move, she mounted him and rode him like a horse. He groaned with pleasure, and his climax was unlike anything he had ever experienced. He soon fell asleep, a smile on his face.

Eleanor, on the other hand, was frustrated and not ready for sleep. She returned to her bed, and using the slipperiness of the sperm he had left in her, she plunged as many fingers as she could into her hungry vagina. It was wet and wonderful. In and out, her fingers slid, moving up and down. She climaxed, then climaxed again, and still, she wasn't satisfied. She wanted the real thing. Eleanor wanted a man between her legs. A man deep inside. Thinking of it, she climaxed again. At last, she slept and dreamed of riding a naked stranger.

Seven

Chapter 7

W hile the Cat is Away.

Harold had yet to make a return visit. Eleanor told herself she had no desire ever to see him again, but the naked man in her dreams wouldn't go away. On the other hand, her husband was there every time she turned around. She was relieved when he received a letter calling for his presence in London. A day or two alone would be delightful.

Lord Edward had left for the city, and Eleanor was alone at last. She had risen that morning, and instead of putting on a corset, she had chosen to wear a loose-fitting garment she had found among his former wife's clothes. How amazing it felt to be free of bondage. Her body could breathe. The servants had been given the day off, and the gardeners were not expected back until Monday. She was alone and could do as she pleased for the first time in a long time.

Eleanor wandered around the house and out into the garden. The air was heavy with the scent of roses. Her hair was loose, and the breeze felt good on her neck. The frizzy hair from yesteryear had disappeared, and in its place lay shiny chestnut ringlets. Eleanor picked a rose and placed it in her hair. Shade beckoned her from beneath an oak tree. "I should have brought a book with me." she thought but was too lazy to return to the house to fetch one. Sitting under the tree, Eleanor removed her shoes and wiggled her toes. The honey bees, busily gathering pollen, soon sang her to sleep.

Something woke her. A shadow was blocking the sunlight. She opened her eyes in fright to find a man standing over her, laughing.

"What do you have against shoes? Do they offend you?"

She knew at once who it was. Harold had appeared from out of nowhere, as he usually did. Eleanor struggled to her feet and then remembered that she was most inappropriately dressed. She clutched the dressing gown around herself as if to hide that fact.

"I am sorry, but my husband is not here. You must excuse my attire. I was not expecting company."

"Your attire, madam, is perfection. You look like a wood nymph. You could bewitch any mortal man, and I am most undoubtedly mortal.

Eleanor felt her face flush and pulled her garment even tighter. Harold reached out and removed the rose from her hair.

"Are you human or a figment from my imagination?"

"I must return to the house. The servants may need my help." Eleanor managed to say.

"I have just come from the house. It is empty."

"My husband will be returning, and I must dress for dinner."

"Your husband is in London, and I doubt he could return tonight." Harold brushed away the tendrils of hair that had blown across her face.

" It is most inappropriate for you to be here. Please leave." Eleanor turned her back and began to walk away.

" Are you sure you want me to leave?" he asked. He reached out and pulled her towards him. His lips were on the back of her neck, his breath scalding her skin. Eleanor became weak in the knees. It was all she could do to remain standing. His hands slid from her shoulders to her breasts. Pulling aside the garment's thin material, he began rubbing her nipples between his fingers. Turning her to face him, he bent and seized a nipple in his mouth. The sensation was overwhelming. Eleanor sunk to the ground.

Her eyes were closed, and her breath came in gasps. Harold kissed her, then returned to her breast, his other hand reaching beneath her skirt till he found what he sought. His finger began stroking her, and then he slipped them inside. Eleanor feared her heart would burst from her body. She found herself moving in rhythm with his fingers, wanting more.

Harold had stopped for a moment to undo his britches. Eleanor cried out in frustration, then Harold's penis penetrated her. As he entered, it hurt. He moved slowly, pacing himself. The discomfort gave way to an incredible sensation. Eleanor moved faster and faster, wanting more. Harold laughed and matched her move for move. The sudden eruption that occurred almost caused her to faint. She lay there, unable to move.

Harold lay beside her, His fingers tracing circles on her stomach. This was unlike anything she had imagined when she pleasured herself. His fingers were once again on her breasts, and her nipples were rising to the occasion. She rolled over and began massaging him. Within minutes, his penis began to swell. Eleanor stared at it with amazement. Seeing one fully erect was frightening.

Harold laughed and pulled her on top of him. Holding her by the waist, he slowly lowered her onto the now stiff member. "Slow," he told her. "Go slow."

Eleanor did as she was told, rising up until his penis was almost free, then slowly sliding down till he filled her completely. She was in control and could go as fast or as slow as she chose to. Harold reached up and pinched her nipples gently. Time stood still. All there was was this slow-moving in and out. Eleanor wanted it to go on forever. Suddenly, the rhythm changed, and she moved faster and faster. Eleanor wanted him deeper and deeper inside her. Her whole body cried out for the explosion she knew was coming.

They lay exhausted. Later, Eleanor might feel guilty, but for now, she lay in blissful, peaceful fulfillment. This stranger, someone she didn't know, had shown her what sex could be. It was Harold who insisted they return to the house and dress. The servants would be returning soon, and there mustn't be a whiff of scandal surrounding Lord Edward's wife.

He was right. Eleanor cared for her husband, and there was no need to hurt him. Harold confessed that he, too, was married. Eleanor was shocked. He had obviously planned her seduction. Why do that if he had a wife? Harold explained that you marry for money and position, which had nothing to do with sex. Initially, he had tried to interest his wife in the pleasures of it, but she declined. There were two children now, a girl and a boy, so she saw no reason to share his bed.

Eleanor questioned him as to why he had chosen her. How

did he know she would be compliant? Harold explained there is an energy around a sensual woman. It will appear unexpectedly. The feeling will be mutual. Sometimes, one would act on it, but sometimes, not. There had been such a strong connection between them from the first time they met it was hard to ignore. He could tell she felt it, too, even if she didn't understand what was happening.

Harold left as quietly as he had appeared. By the time the servants returned, she had eaten a cold supper and retired to her chambers. Upon his return, her husband would find a devoted wife. All is well that ends well.

Eight

Chapter 8

Taking Care of Lord Edward.

The next morning, Eleanor experienced waves of guilt and fear. "How could she have been so careless? The servants could have come back early or, worse, her husband. He had been nothing but a kind and loving man, and she had betrayed him." She could blame Harold, but, in truth, she had never tried to stop him, but encouraged his every move. Even as she scolded herself, her body remembered everything.

"This must never happen again." She would forget Harold and concentrate on her marriage. Why had she given in to her foolish urges? Eleanor resolved to be a perfect wife.

Lord Edward had returned from London with a bad cold that soon turned into pneumonia. The doctor was called and predicted a dire outcome. Eleanor bathed him with vinegar water, rubbed his hands and feet, placed mustered plasters on his back and chest, and never left his side for days. When he began to show signs of improvement, she plied him with herbal tea and chicken soup. She wept, believing this was punishment for her wicked actions.

Mary Clair came to help. She found her brother much better, but his wife was exhausted. She sent Eleanor to bed, aired out the house and the bedclothes, and settled in to talk with her brother. It was clear to her that Eleanor had risked her own health to care for Edward.

"Edward," she began, " If you realize how close you came to dying and would have without the care of your young wife, it's time to do something about it. I have explained to you what was done to protect me from harm. Eleanor would have lost everything if you had passed, and some long-lost relative would have come crawling out of the woodwork to claim it all. Now that I am sure she isn't a gold digger, I would encourage you to do for her what my husband did for me. Give her ownership of everything by selling it to her. It cost me a pound for each of the properties I acquired, including the house. Have the deeds notarized by a magistrate. Please do this for Eleanor as soon as possible."

Edward trusted his sister and considered everything she told him. Mary Clair was right. Why should some stranger claim everything he owned? There was, as yet, no son to inherit it all. If they were lucky enough to have a boy, a wife's property would pass to her son. Mary Clair showed him her documents, and he copied them word for word. He would visit his solicitor and then present the papers to a judge as soon as he was able to travel.

Eleanor was so exhausted that all thoughts of Harold were forgotten. She slept for hours, knowing her husband was in the capable hands of her sister-in-law. She had yet to learn about the legal business that was taking place while she slept. Each time she woke, Mary Clair was there with tea and chicken soup. Her strength slowly returned.

Nine

Chapter 9

Slow Decline.

Lord Edward and his wife were off to London to shop for new gowns and visit his solicitor. He felt much better and intended to file copies of the document at the courthouse. Eleanor was shocked and upset to find that he intended to give her all he had. It only added to her guilt. Her misery was made worse, if that was possible, when her monthly flow was late. Her husband had been too ill since he had arrived home for it to be his child. That only left one other person. Eleanor lived in hell until, at last, her blood showed. This only stiffened her resolve never to be unfaithful again.

The couple purchased fabric and visited a dressmaker. They attended the theater and visited with friends of Lord Edward's before presenting their papers at the courthouse. After several fittings at the dressmakers and completing their legal business, they returned home. The garments would be sent on as soon as they were finished. Eleanor found it impossible to express her gratitude for Edward's generosity. She discovered how very much she cared for this man when he nearly died.

Weeks passed, and there had been no sign of Harold. That had made her resolve never to be unfaithful to Edward again so much easier. Her will was strong. She did her best to put all thoughts of that day in the garden out of her mind, but it didn't stop the wild dreams that filled her nights.

Eleanor soon realized Edward was not himself. Even though he had made a complete recovery from pneumonia, his energy had suffered. Special foods were prepared. Bone broth and other things to strengthen him were given daily and their time together had changed. They would lay in bed, and he would tell her stories of his days in boarding school, his many trips, or he would read to her from the books in his library. He had no interest in her body.

Eleanor could sign her name or read simple things, but her father had seen no need to educate girls, especially his youngest daughter. Lord Edward made sure she could now understand the ledgers and do much more than write her name. He included her when meeting with his accountant or the rent collector.

While she struggled with reading and writing, the numbers came quickly. Eleanor had been responsible for keeping track of the animals on her father's estate. With them being sold off at an alarming rate, it was easy to see when one was missing.

One day, she questioned a discrepancy in the number of sheep on the books after some were taken to market. The new lambs should have been added. The accountant was upset at her interference, but Lord Edward would have none of it. Eleanor was to be respected and listened to, or the accountant would be replaced. The man left in a foul mood but never made that mistake again.

Week after week, Edward grew weaker. He had a hard time moving from bed to chair, and then there came a time when he chose to remain in bed. Eleanor sent for Mary Clair.

The two women took turns feeding him and helping him sip herbal teas or heated Brandy. Hot water bottles were placed in his bed to warm him. The doctor and priest came and went. There was nothing to do but wait.

Edward dozed on and off. The two women who loved him lay beside him in the large bed. Mary Clair spoke of childhood pranks he played, telling funny tales that made him smile. They sang silly nursery rhymes and took turns massaging his feet and hands.

When he passed, they remained there, holding his hands until the sun came up. The women dressed and went downstairs to notify the household that Lord Edward was dead.

Mary Clair took charge of everything. It was she who notified the priest, the doctor, and his solicitor. Arrangements were made to open the family crypt. Lord Edward was laid to rest beside his first wife. Once again, extra servants were hired to care for all the guests who came for the funeral.

It was Mary Clair who shepherded a numb Eleanor through it all. Eleanor came and went as instructed, like a trained dog. The doctor gave her something to make her sleep, and Mary Clair forced her to eat, but all she wanted was for everyone to go away and leave her alone with her grief.

Ten

Chapter 10

A Gift.

A month had passed since Edward's death, and Mary Clair had returned home. Eleanor hated the empty house. The garden was the only place she felt alive. She would work there, sometimes digging in the dirt herself. She even set up a table in the courtyard where she would work on the books. Eleanor found that emerging herself in the numbers, making them all match, took her mind off her loss for a little while. Every day seemed longer than the one before

A widow has little social life. Eleanor would be in mourning for a year. It was what was expected of her. The loneliness did nothing to repair her aching heart. She missed Edward. Her father had passed the year before from a heart attack, leaving his debtors to scramble for what was left of his holdings. Eleanor had barely noticed his death, but Lord Edward's death had left a huge hole in her heart.

One day, a crate was delivered to the house without a note or information as to who had sent it. When the gardener opened it for her, a pair of fur balls fell out. The tiny pups, released from their prison, rolled over and over in the grass. All Eleanor could do was laugh at their antics.

Who had given her such a delightful gift? Someone had understood how alone she felt and sent the pups to ease her grief. A large cushion was placed beside the bed. That was where they were to sleep. After listening to their whimpering, she gave up and lifted them into the bed, where they soon snuggled under the covers and fell asleep. Eleanor was awakened in the morning by wiggly bodies and wet tongues.

The dogs grew by leaps and bounds. The stable boy had been recruited to train them. Penny and Pudgy adored their mistress and were never far from her side. Having them helped her heart heal and make time go faster. Six months after Lord Edward's death, Eleanor, with dogs in tow, decided to visit her sister-in-law.

Chapter 11

An Amazing Revelation.

Eleanor couldn't wait any longer, so she set out a day earlier than expected. Upon arrival, she was told she would find her sister-in-law on the back terrace. Eleanor left the pups with the maid and hurried through the house to the garden. She opened the French doors to the terrace in time to see a tall, handsome, white-haired gentleman mount his horse and ride away down the back garden path.

Mary Clair lay on the wicker lounge, a drink in one hand and a half-smoked cigar in the other. She wore a delicate thin robe of lavender muslin, and her loose hair moved freely in the breeze. An empty glass and a snubbed-out cigar sat on the table beside the other chair. Eleanor was at a loss for words. Her sister-in-law had been entertaining a man in a very intimate setting. Who was he, and why had he been here?

Seeing the look on Eleanor's face, Mary Clair laughed. "You have arrived earlier than I expected. Don't look so shocked. I am old, not dead. I was entertaining a long-time friend and lover. He and I were young together, and now we see each other often. The fire of youth has burned out, but the warm embers are most delightful."

Eleanor managed to stammer out, "Your lover?"

"Are you surprised to find that I am still interested in such things? Just because one's husband dies does not mean I must shrivel up and waste away. It is time you consider what you will do with the rest of your life. Your husband left you independent. You can do whatever you choose. If you are foolish enough to marry, a man will claim all you have, and you will be helpless to do anything about it."

" What are you saying?"

"You don't need to be alone. You don't need to marry. I have been waiting to have this talk with you. The time has come a little faster than I had anticipated. Let us go into supper and discuss these things later."

Eleanor followed her into the house. The dogs were delighted to find another human to entertain them, but their antics couldn't distract Eleanor from Mary Clair's revelation. She had always admired her sister-in-law's good sense. Now, she was seeing a whole new side of Mary Clair that she never realized existed.

The dogs lay snoozing by the fire. The servant had retired for the evening, and the two women were alone. Mary Clair had poured them a brandy and began.

" Men think they are the only ones entitled to have sex outside of marriage. The idea that women would have desires and want sexual experiences, and perhaps with more than one lover, would shock them. You need a lover, a man who will make you feel alive. It isn't necessary to be in love or marry, but to be discreet. Avoid scandal and pregnancy at all costs."

Eleanor stared at Mary Clair in disbelief. What was her sister-in-law suggesting? That she take a lover? Or more than one? Women grew up and married. The only other choice was to be an old maid or a nun. If you were widowed and had no children, you did charity work and lived alone till you died.

"You have an advantage that most widows do not. You are financially independent. Do not bother unpacking. Tomorrow, we will leave the dogs in the care of the staff, and you and I are making a visit to Bath, the wonderfully restorative spa. Even though you are officially still in mourning, it will be acceptable as you will be traveling with your sister-in-law. No one will think unkindly about such a thing. You are going there for health reasons."

"Why would I do such a thing, and what does that have to do with our conversation? I am confused and confounded by everything you are saying." Eleanor had always trusted Mary Clair, but perhaps her brother's death had damaged her sister-in-law's power of reason.

Mary Clair rose and kissed Eleanor's cheek. "Have a good night's sleep. We will leave early tomorrow morning. I shall enjoy introducing you to the pleasures available in Bath. The waters are most invigorating." Having said that, Mary Clair left the room, leaving Eleanor speechless. She retired to her bed but found it hard to sleep. The day had been full of unbelievable surprises.

II

Part Two

Lessons Learned

Twelve

Chapter 12

B ath
They arrived at the hotel in Bath and were escorted to an apartment with a sitting room, two bedrooms, and a dressing room. Their luggage was delivered, and a lady's maid arrived to unpack their clothing. They rested, washed up, and went down to lunch.

After lunch, they took a stroll out into the gardens, admiring the beautiful ground surrounding the hotel. Mary Clair announced they had an appointment for a private bath at the mineral spring and a massage. Eleanor wasn't sure exactly what that was or whether she wanted one. She had always trusted Mary Clair, but since the startling revelations the day before, Eleanor wasn't sure what to expect.

Upon their arrival at the women's bathhouse, the concierge greeted Mary Clair with delight. He informed them that everything had been arranged as usual and led them to a changing room. A maid instructed Eleanor to disrobe completely and put on the dressing gown provided. She did as instructed and waited nervously for what was next.

The maid returned and led her to a private room with a large bathtub filled with scented mineral water. The woman removed the robe and helped her into the tub.

Eleanor had never been naked before a stranger and was rather uncomfortable, but the warm rose-scented water and the gentle scrubbing soon relaxed her, and she succumbed to the sensation and could have stayed there for hours. She reluctantly rose from the bath, and after being wrapped in a large towel, she was led to the adjoining room.

Once there, Eleanor was instructed to lie face down on a table and was covered with a sheet. With trepidation, she did as she was told. A woman entered the room and began massaging her body with lavender-scented oil. Up and down her back, then across the shoulders, the woman's hands moved, searching for the places on her body that needed attention. At last, her legs and then her feet were rubbed. It was unlike anything she had ever experienced. She had been relaxed in the tub, but this was amazing. When the woman asked her to turn over, it was all she could do to comply.

The massaging continued. Her shoulders and neck were treated, leaving Eleanor feeling as if there were no bones in her body. She barely managed to thank the masseuse for everything before the smiling woman left the room.

Eleanor lay on the table in a state of euphoria, not wishing to move. Someone was rubbing her feet. "How lovely," she thought," The masseuse had come back." She didn't bother to open her eyes.

The hands moved up her legs to her hips. How strange, now her shoulders, too, were being rubbed. She must be dreaming. There couldn't be two sets of hands. The fingers moved lower until they cradled her breasts, then began to pinch her nipples lightly. The hands on her hips had moved down and now circled her most private parts. They began to rub her lips gently, then spread them to reach the soft raised place between. Her nipples were being sucked, and still half asleep, she spread her legs.

The sensation of the two actions was incredible. Eleanor had never had such an erotic dream. Now, the fingers were inside, moving in and out. Her nipples were hard from the licking and gentle biting. Eleanor felt a climax coming. Suddenly, she was lifted from the table to a couch.

Startled, she opened her eyes. Two men smiled at her. Eleanor gasped. This was real, not a dream. How could this be happening? She was ready to cry out, but now the blond man placed his head between her legs and began sucking her clit while the second man sucked her nipples.

It was impossible to stop them even if she wanted to, and she didn't want to. What she wanted was for this experience never to end. Every nerve in her body was more awake than it had ever been. She climaxed, but soon, she was ready to climax again.

The blond pulled her onto his lap. He lowered her slowly onto his stiff penis. The second man began to rock her back and forth on the enormous cock while twisting her nipples. The massive erection filled her, while at the same time, the rocking motion rubbed against her clit. Her climax began at the bottom of her feet and exploded throughout her body. Eleanor swooned and collapsed in a heap.

Lowering her to the couch, the men bathed her private parts

with warm, damp towels and helped her into her robe. They kissed her, and after thanking her for the delightful afternoon, they suggested she ask for them if she visited the establishment again.

"What had they said? Revisit? Ask for them?" Eleanor thought, "Had this all been arranged beforehand?" Mary Clair was the only one who could have done that. Eleanor wasn't sure how to react. Should she thank her or be angry? As soon as she was able to, she returned to their rooms and fell asleep until Mary Clair woke her with a cup of somewhat bitter tea.

Thirteen

Chapter 13

H ome.

The next day, Eleanor was happy to use the public hot springs to ease the soreness she was experiencing. Thinking back on all that had happened, she became hot all over. It had been unlike anything she had ever dreamed of. Had Mary Clair ordered everything that had taken place, and had she, too, shared a similar experience? Was there even more to her sister-in-law than she had imagined?

Mary Clair had asked her if she had a good day yesterday but had yet to say a word about whether or not she had arranged the whole thing. Eleanor was too embarrassed to broach the subject. It seemed wiser to leave it alone.

The next day, they left for Mary Clair's estate. Eleanor would be glad to see the dogs, and she was ready to return home. They spoke of mundane things on the way and never mentioned what had happened at the hot springs. Eleanor was not sure that everything had been Mary Clair's doing. What if it hadn't been arranged by her sister-in-law? She was afraid to ask.

Two excited balls of fur greeted the women. It had been their mistress's first absence since they had been delivered to her, and the dogs were ecstatic. They barked and ran in circles, both trying to sit on her lap at once.

"Dogs are so loving and loyal. You never need to doubt their love. Wouldn't it be wonderful if men were as trustworthy?" Mary Clair sighed. "It is sad to think that one must always be on guard when it comes to money and property. Soon, men will be beating down your door with promises of fidelity and undying devotion. Not only are you rich, but you are also beautiful. Trust no one. Play the man's game. Smile and flirt, but hold on tightly to your purse strings and your heart,"

They ate a lovely supper and played cards till it was time for bed. Once again, Mary Clair prepared a cup of the bitter tea for her.

Days earlier, when she arrived at Mary Clair's, she could never have imagined anything close to what had happened in Bath. By noon the next day, Eleanor was packed, and the dogs were in their crate, ready to go home. Before leaving, Eleanor invited her sister-in-law to call on her soon, and Mary Clair had promised to do so.

Mary Clair suggested they could travel to London as soon as Eleanor's official morning period was over or perhaps pay a return visit to Bath. She gave her a pouch full of tea, saying," It would be wise to keep it on hand should you have an encounter. A cup of this tea taken for three days will prevent unwanted problems, so be sure to have your third one this evening."

Leaving for home, Eleanor had no doubts as to who had

arranged the experience at the spa.

Fourteen

Chapter 14

Planning for the Future.

Eleanor had hired a teacher to help her improve her reading skills. It hadn't been easy, but being able to read the books in Edward's library gave her a great deal of enjoyment and helped the time pass faster. The most interesting books were those about different countries. How wonderful it would be to visit some of those places. As a woman, traveling alone would be dangerous and definitely frowned on. What if she chose a traveling companion? Who better than her sister-in-law?

Thinking back to her last visit with Mary Clair, could those things she remembered have really happened? Eleanor would never in her wildest dreams believe such things could take place before having the experience in Bath. Was that a specialty of the spa for those who knew the right services to ask for? What other secrets did Mary Clair have to share?

Soon, her official time of mourning would be over. Eleanor loved her home, but a trip to a foreign country would be exciting. There was a ferry that would take you to France, and she had seen photos of huge ocean-going ships that traveled even further. What an adventure it would be to spend weeks on one. Eleanor wrote to Mary Clair and immediately suggested that they consider making such a trip this coming summer. Traveling with her sister-in-law might add to her education in more ways than one.

The reply she received was all she could have wished for. Her sister-in-law would be delighted to accompany her on a grand tour of Europe. As a young woman, Mary Clair, chaperoned by her mother and aunt, had visited both France and Italy. Later, as a new bride, she had been to the French Riviera and Monaco.

How different it would be as independent women. Mary Clair had friends in Europe, and the two women would be most welcome. She would write letters to everyone that she knew in Paris, and they would be expecting the ladies to visit in the late spring. Lady Eleanor had a great deal to look forward to.

Fifteen

Chapter 15

A Visit to France.

The two women departed from Dover and arrived in Calais in the middle of a rain storm. The crossing had been rough, and the train was damp and overcrowded. They had been forced to share a compartment with several other passengers. By the time they reached Paris, they were exhausted. After a light supper and a hot bath, they retired to the adjoining bedrooms for an early night's sleep.

The next morning, after breakfast, Mary Clair hired a horse-drawn cab to take them on a sightseeing tour of the city. She pointed out the wonders of Paris. That evening, after a delightful meal at one of Paris's best restaurants, they attended the latest play. Before retiring for the night, they had a glass of wine in the hotel lobby and enjoyed the quartet playing there. Eleanor thanked her sister-in-law for a beautiful day.

Mary Clair arranged for a visit to a naughty cabaret the following evening, and because ladies were not supposed to attend such a show, they wore plain clothing and large hats with veils. Being incognito made it even more exciting. They pulled the curtain surrounding their box almost shut so as not to call attention to themselves and settled in to watch.

The male crowd was loud and boisterous, whistling and cheering for the nearly naked women on the stage. The dancers were doing something called a can-can with high kicks, made all the more interesting because, under their ruffled dresses, they wore only the scantiest of panties. Eleanor was fascinated by a dancer who used large fans in such a way as to hide and then reveal her body. Tiny fancy patches covered her nipples and private parts. Every lady Eleanor knew hid their bodies with corsets and undergarments. She had never seen a female body in all its glory. "How beautiful." she thought. There was nothing vulgar or ugly about it. It gave her a whole new respect for her own body. When a comedian came on stage and began a very obscene parody, the two women left.

The next few days were filled with shopping and sightseeing. They stopped by an apothecary shop known to Mary Clair and purchased a container full of the bitter tea that would keep trouble from the door if a woman preferred not to have a child.

Mary Clair's European friends soon became Eleanor's friends, and invitations to gatherings poured in. A beautiful or rich woman was always welcome, and Eleanor was both. A hand-some Russian Count was particularly attentive. His manners were impeccable, and he was an excellent dancer. Within a week, Count Alexei had declared his undying love for her. Eleanor was flattered by his amorous attentions but had been warned by Mary Clair. He was not only a notorious gambler who had lost all his money but a man who would kiss and tell. Eleanor thanked him but stated that she was still mourning her late husband and not interested.

He was not the only man that found Eleanor attractive. Mary Clair would tease her, declaring that their suite was beginning to resemble a florist shop. The calling cards piled up on the sitting room desk, and the two ladies never lacked for escorts, but the time had come to leave Paris.

A compartment had been booked on the train to Nice for the next day, and a large masquerade party was planned for that evening to bid them farewell. Several gentlemen offered to travel with them for security, but the ladies politely declined. The best part of this adventure was that they were free to do and be whatever they wished. The last thing they needed was some male to cramp their style.

Mary Clair had dressed as a nun, which amused Eleanor no end because of what she had learned about her sister-in-law. Eleanor wanted to dress as the fan dancer from the burlesque, but she knew that was impossible, so she chose to be a Spanish Flamenco dancer. The many ruffles of the skirt reminded her of the naughty can-can dancers. No one else would understand their choice of costumes, but both she and Mary Clair laughed at their shared secret. The ladies put on their masques and went to join the party.

Chapter 16

A Masked Man

Count Alexei was becoming a nuisance. When Eleanor danced with someone else, he pouted and glared at them until the dance was over and then rushed over to beg her for the next dance. When he wasn't looking, she slipped out into the solarium.

Choosing a hidden corner behind some large palm trees, she sat down and began fanning herself. The ruffled full skirt was hot around her legs. A wicked thought crossed her mind. She stood up, slid her pantaloons off, and stuffed them into a larger garden cart that stood nearby. If the gardener should sort through the trash, he would be in for a big surprise.

Feeling very naughty, Eleanor wandered into the garden. She was extremely aware of her naked pussy. The sensation made her want to pleasure herself. She stood by the raised fountain, trailing her hand through the water. Suddenly, someone's hands were around her waist. She assumed angrily that it was the Count until a familiar voice said, "I see you have your shoes on for a change."

She turned to see a highwayman with a mask and a long black cape. Eleanor had no doubt as to the speaker's identity. She turned her back to him. "I haven't seen you in a year or more, and now here you are in Europe. I told you that you should be belled like a cat so you couldn't sneak up on people."

Harold pulled her to him and began nuzzling the back of her neck. "You have grown even more beautiful since the last time we met, if that is even possible." His hands moved up to her bodice. "This dress has too many hooks and eyes. It would take too long to free these beauties."

Eleanor was trying to ignore him, but through the material of her dress, her nipples were growing hard. He reached down and seized the front of her skirt, Soon it was up around her waist. "Why, you wicked woman! You seem to have lost your panties." Both hands were now reaching between her legs. Against her will, she opened them. His fingers found what they were searching for. He rubbed the lips, then spread them so he could rub her clit. The fingers of his other hand were soon inside her. She needed to lean against him to keep her balance.

"Oh, you sweet girl. You are so wet. Tell me how you love this. Do you want it? My britches are open. Reach back and see what I have for you."

Eleanor reached back, and her hand found his member. It was stiff and hard against her." Rub it, rub it for me." He groaned with pleasure. " Oh, God! I've got to have you. Pull up the back of your skirt and bend over the edge of the fountain."

Harold pulled the black cloak around them, grabbed her, and pulled her backward onto his cock. With his fingers still rubbing her clit, he drove again and again into her wet pussy. The fingers created friction on her clit, and the hard prick filled her cunt. Eleanor had been pleasuring herself since her visit to Bath. She had forgotten just how good having the real thing inside her could feel. She climaxed, then climaxed again, and still wanted more. Harold gave a loud groan, and then his pulsing cock spewed forth its load. "Please don't stop, I want more." Harold laughed, then put his fingers inside her pussy, still dripping from his ejaculation, and brought her to the brink of climax again. Her moans caused his cock to grow hard once more. When he removed his fingers, she cried out in disappointment. Those cries were soon replaced by moans of delight when his engorged prick pushed deep into her hungry cunt. She matched him stroke for stroke until they both reached the peak and exploded.

After they had begun to breathe normally and had restored their clothing to a somewhat proper state, Harold had suggested they could meet again the next day. Eleanor would have loved a repeat performance, but Mary Clair had booked tickets on the early train the next day. If he could find her in Paris, perhaps he might find her in the south of France.

" With or without nickers," he said laughing.

Seventeen

Chapter 17

N

ice.

After rearranging her costume and tidying her hair, she returned to the ballroom and sought out Mary Clair. Much to Count Alexei's disappointment, they said their goodbyes and were soon on their way back to the hotel. Eleanor hadn't said a thing about what had happened in the garden, but from the look on Mary Clair's face, she was pretty sure her sister-in-law had a good idea of what had taken place. When she made herself a cup of the bitter tea,a it confirmed everything that Mary Clair suspected.

The trip to Nice was to be a time to rest and relax. Mary Clair knew no one there, so there would be no social obligations to fill their days. Eleanor thought back to the last night she had spent in Paris, the sudden appearance of Harold, and all that had taken place because of it. Other than the amazing experience in Bath, she had never been with a man. You couldn't count the clumsy sexual efforts of her husband as dear as he was.

Their hotel in Nice was nice even if the beach was rocks instead of sand, and the bathing dresses were hot and heavy when wet. They strode the promenade, shopped for perfume, and in the evenings, they often went to Monaco to the newly opened Place du Casino in Monte Carlo. They were not big gamblers but enjoyed playing the tables. Several gentlemen had shown an interest in the lovely British ladies. While Mary Clair was not young, she still had the ability to attract male attention. There was an unexplained aura of sensuality that surrounded both women.

Just as in Paris, their hotel room was soon filled with calling cards and flowers. They never lacked escorts. Single men on the Riviera were a mixed bag. There were playboys, with and without money, titled gentlemen seeking a dalliance, professional gigolos, widowers seeking new wives, or gay young men who made excellent escorts because they made no sexual demands at the end of the evening. While it was fun to be flattered and fawned over, none of them aroused Eleanor's interest. A visit from Harold would be welcomed.

Eighteen

Chapter 18

Visit to the Beach.

Eleanor could tell that something was going on. Mary Clair had been distracted throughout dinner and suggested they skip dessert and return to their rooms. Once there, she retrieved a package from the cupboard and opened it. Inside were skirts and blouses, not unlike the clothing the peasant women wore.

"Tonight, we are going to join the underground life here on the Riviera. No fancy clothes or hair. Take off your jewelry and brush your hair out. "

Eleanor did as she was told, and after dressing and adding shawls and scarves, they slipped down the back stairs of the hotel and out into the street. Arriving at a beach side cafe, they ordered a glass of wine and soon were invited to join a group of local drinkers at the next table.

Several drinks later, someone at the table suggested that the two of them would be a welcome part of the night's revelry. Everyone was going to one of the underground clubs. Would they like to go with them? Mary Clair and Eleanor were first blindfolded, and then they were taken from the cafe and led down some steps. After a long walk with twists and turns and passing through what could have been a tunnel, they arrived at a door. A password was muttered, and their blindfolds were removed. They found themselves inside a massive cave full of people all dancing and drinking.

Their guides introduced the two women and they were soon an accepted part of the party. Max, the man who seemed to be the leader of the group, was tanned and extremely well-built. While no one would call him handsome, an animal magnetism surrounded him. There were drinks other than wine, and Eleanor found herself drinking something called Pernod Absinthe. It tasted like licorice, and her glass was filled several times. She was glad to have strong arms to help her balance when invited to dance.

Soon, they were passing around cigarettes with a strange odor. Eleanor knew that Mary Clair smoked cigars, but she had never smoked anything. A deep draw on the cigarette caused her to cough, and she had a hard time stopping. She decided to forgo smoking.

Eleanor was beginning to feel light-headed. Fresh air would help, so she rose and headed towards a side door. It seemed so far away. She felt as though she was walking through water. Many members of the group joined her, including Max. Once outside, she realized that the cave door opened onto a beach. The fresh air helped a little, but she felt disconnected, as if her head was detached from her body. Maybe a splash in the sea would help. Eleanor began removing her clothes.

When the others saw what she was doing, they, too, stripped. Soon, everyone was naked and happily splashing around in the surf. Eleanor dreamed of her trips to the river as a girl. The cold seawater stung, and her nipples hardened. Hands were rubbing them and then her private parts. She found herself mounted on someone's cock, her legs wrapped around the man's hips. With the motion of the waves and the motion of the large organ inside her, she climaxed. The strong hands surrounding her waist belonged to Max. He carried her to the beach without removing her from his engorged member. He knelt on a rug someone had laid there and gently lowered her upper torso. Holding her that way, with her legs on his shoulders so that he could thrust deeper into her, he continued his action. He would withdraw until he was on the brink of exiting, then slowly enter her till he filled her completely. Eleanor lost count of how many times she had an orgasm. She would think there was no way she could have another. Still, then the pleasure would begin to rise inside her once more because of Max's ever-persistent penetration into her hungry vagina with his fantastic dick, and the explosion would happen again. Then, when Max could no longer hold back, with a loud groan, he too climaxed.

Someone had brought a blanket to the beach, and one by one, people emerged from the sea. A fire had been built, and after warming up and drying off, people were putting on their clothes and leaving. Eleanor's head had begun to clear, and Max helped her dress. He kissed her and slapped her on the backside. It was time to go. The night sky was showing signs of fading. She needed to find Mary Clair and return to the hotel while it was still dark.

Chapter 18

Nineteen

Chapter 19

An Unpleasant Encounter and a Lesson Learned.

As wonderful as their adventure to the club had been, the ladies decided it would be unwise to chance such a thing again. As much as hotel staff gossiped, there was always the fear of being exposed as the adventurous women they were. They must appear to be the proper aristocratic British widows everyone thought them to be. No scandal must touch them.

The women were becoming bored with the social scene in Nice. The men were all about as exciting as dead fish. Harold had not shown up, and Max was nowhere in sight, and even if he was, would he recognize Eleanor as the wanton woman from the beach?

Mary Clair suggested they move on to the Spanish Riviera or Italy, or they could backtrack and catch the Orient Express. Eleanor was game for either of these, so they flipped a coin, and the Orient Express won. They would need to return to Paris to catch the famous train. A few days spent in Paris would be welcome. Perhaps Harold would still be there.

Their arrival in Paris was met with enthusiasm by their friend, who promptly used their presence as an excuse to throw a party, not that they ever needed one. The evening was in full swing, a jazz combo, the latest craze in the famous city was happily playing for the crowd. Eleanor and Mary Clair were regaling their friends with imitations of the men they had met in the south of France when Eleanor saw a couple enter the apartment. She recognized the man immediately. It was Harold. Who was the woman with him?

Eleanor was finding it hard to breathe. How could Harold be here with someone? Was this woman the reason he hadn't followed them to Nice? She couldn't believe she felt so jealous. After all, she had always known that Harold had other women, and had she not been experiencing sex with other men? Eleanor pasted a smile on her face and tried to pay attention to the person speaking to her. What she wanted to do was run over and scratch Harold's eyes out.

The couple toured the room, stopping to chat with several people, and finally reached their host. Harold introduced the woman as his wife. She had arrived weeks earlier on a surprise visit. She had come to Paris on a shopping trip and to check up on her husband. While she might not wish to share his bed, she didn't want any rumors to mar the appearance of a happy marriage.

"His wife!" Eleanor had always known that he had a wife. He had told her so. She, too, had been married when they had first met, but seeing the woman was different from just hearing about her. Harold would be off-limits from now on.

Eleanor had drank too much and laughed and flirted the night away. Who cared if Harold was here in Paris; he meant nothing to her. The following day, she was too ill to go to lunch with Mary Clair and her friends. All she wanted was to sleep and forget everything, especially Harold.

After lunch, she had the maid bring her a cup of coffee and draw her a bath. The coffee helped her headache, and the soak in the hot tub was relaxing. When the door opened, Eleanor rose from the tub and soon found herself wrapped in a large, warm towel. "How nice of the maid." she thought, " I must give her something extra."

Strong arms picked her up and carried her to the bed. Eleanor tried to cry out, but a hand was clamped across her mouth.

"Oh, my sweet girl, how I have missed you. I was ready to follow you to Nice when my wife appeared at the hotel."

Eleanor bit his hand and shouted at him. " Your wife! How dear you come here. I never want to see you again. Do you think you can just come here and act as if nothing was wrong? Get out!"

Harold stopped her from speaking by kissing her lips and then her neck. He caught her hand as she tried to slap him and moved it to his stiff member. "Do you think I get stiff like this for her? It's you I want to be inside. Deep inside that sweet pussy." He began sucking on her nipples and rubbing her clit. "Oh, feel how you want this. Feel how much you want me deep inside you. Let me show you."

Harold began kissing her breasts and her stomach, and then he spread her legs and kissed her sweet spot. His tongue lapped at her pussy. He sucked and nibbled till she cried out and climaxed. Harold laughed and began again. Eleanor whimpered and begged him to enter her. He teased her, saying," You didn't want anything to do with me, and now you are begging me. It's your turn to prove how much you want it. Rub me, and lick me. Make me so big and hard you will have trouble mounting me."

Harold lay back on the bed, and Eleanor knelt between his legs and took his member in her hands. She pushed back on the soft skin around it and licked the head of his penis. He moaned with pleasure. She rubbed the shaft and licked it several times, then she put it in her mouth and sucked. Harold cried out and gripped her head. Eleanor had never felt such power. Eleanor fondled his balls while she sucked and licked his dick until he couldn't take it anymore. He pulled her onto his swollen rod, and she rode him until they both came with such force they couldn't breathe.

They rested, but Eleanor wanted to try the new trick she had learned and soon began rubbing and licking Harold's member. He was becoming stiff again and pulled her on top of him, but now she was facing his feet. Eleanor could suck his dick while he could lick her sweet pussy. He spread her labia so he could suck on her clit, and she would lick the tip of his prick, then slide the whole thing into her mouth and suck. When they could stand it no longer, he turned her over and pulled her up on her knees. Kneeling and entering her wet vagina from behind, Harold fucked her hard and deep, rubbing her clitoris with one hand and her nipples with the other. Their climax was incredible.

They lay there exhausted but happy. Eleanor had forgotten all thoughts of never being with him again. She had also learned something about herself that she had never realized before. She enjoyed being in complete control and making a man half crazy with what she had just learned to do. With her husband, she had discovered the first lesson about the power of sex, and now she had graduated to the head of the class. Let Harold's wife match that!

Twenty

Chapter 20

The Trip Must Wait.

A letter had been left at the hotel for Mary Clair. Her caregiver at her estate had become ill. He had been with her for many years, and she trusted him completely. There would be no one to replace him. Mary Clair must leave for England immediately.

As much as she was looking forward to another meeting with Harold, it would be unwise for Eleanor to remain in Europe alone, and she did miss her little fur babies. Penny and Pudgy were no longer pups, and sadly, dogs didn't live as long as one would wish. The Orient Express would be laying new tracks, and in a year or two, it would be going even further than Budapest. There was no reason to believe that the next year would not see them returning and booking such a trip. It was time to go home. She would check on her estate to be sure all was well there.

How much fun it would be to plan and dream of all the new adventures awaiting them. While Harold would be a frequent diversion, there were always visits to Bath. Who knows, Mary Clair might have a few more secrets up her sleeve. Eleanor could have never imagined all she had experienced since that first cold lesson in the river as a young girl.

After bidding their friends goodbye, the ladies booked their passage home. They were impatient to arrive and check on everything. Mary Clair was relieved to find her caregiver greatly improved. His son had been of service while the gentleman had been indisposed. She suggested that the son be given a new position as his father's assistant and that he be schooled in the care of the estate so as to aid his father and be prepared to take over when his father retired. It was important to have persons that one could trust in such positions.

Eleanor was greeted by two ecstatic dogs. She remembered what Mary Clair had said about dogs being more faithful than people. Her dogs might be getting up in age, but that didn't stop them from running in circles and barking with joy. They had been a blessing when she had lost her husband and a comfort in those lonely days. They had missed her so much. They were growing old, and it didn't seem fair to leave them for more than a day or two now. If it was a short trip, she could take them with her when she went to visit.

Perhaps she would stay in England until her four-legged babies were gone. Eleanor would take this time to handle any repairs the estate needed and to confer with her solicitors. It was best to consider what should happen to everything at her demise. Her only living relatives were her sisters, but she had been estranged from them for many years.

III

Part Three

A Family Gathering

Twenty-One

Chapter 21

Perhaps It Was Time.

Eleanor had been home for some time. Some additions to the garden had been made, and a leak in the roof had been repaired. The dogs were growing old. Pudgy had lost his eyesight but had adjusted to it and followed his litter mate around. There had been another visit to Bath, and Harold met with her whenever he could. Mary Clair had fallen and broken her arm before Christmas, and their plans to take the trip on the Orient Express had to be put off once again.

Lady Eleanor felt that it was time to visit her solicitor to discuss the disposition of her estate. Neither she nor Mary Clair had children, and Eleanor's deceased husband had no relatives. One never knew when something might happen, and Mary Clair's fall had reminded her of that. Eleanor had siblings, of course, but they had never been close.

Her sisters had always been happy to look down on her as their poor relative, but then, Eleanor's station in life had changed. Suddenly, she was rich, owned a large estate, and had a title. That just wasn't fair. Their jealousy wouldn't let them be friends. She knew there were nieces and nephews, but she had never met them. Perhaps it was time to make an effort to do so. Eleanor would arrange an afternoon tea in London and send out invitations to the families. It would be interesting to see who, if anyone, would reply.

Some had angrily torn up the invitations, but others, intrigued by an invitation from Lady Eleanor decided to attend especially the youngsters. Many of them never knew they had an aunt. Their parents had never mentioned a younger sister and certainly not one who had married a Lord. One or two of her sisters were curious to see what their ugly duckling sibling looked like after so many years.

A private dining room had been set aside for the tea. The hotel had gone all out to make everything perfect, with linen tablecloths, beautiful china, and crystal glasses. Silver tea services and delicate sandwiches and cakes decorated every table. White-gloved waiters stood around, ready to anticipate their every need. The families gathered and pretended not to be impressed by such a display. They awaited Eleanor's appearance.

Eleanor's hair had been simply dressed, and while her dress was the latest in fashion, she had taken great pains not to appear too rich or glamorous. The group stared at her. How could this elegant creature be their relative? Gone was the awkward, frizzy-haired girl. She had been replaced by a poised, graceful, chestnut-haired beauty, and the intervening years had been much kinder to her than to her sisters.

Eleanor moved from table to table, introducing herself to these long-lost family members. While they all were polite, some were cold and unfriendly, but others seemed interested in getting to know this strange woman who had suddenly made an appearance in their lives. Several of her nephews were in advanced studies at university, and a niece was engaged to be married. For the most part, the young people were her best audience.

One sister was widowed, one had died, and the other four who had chosen to come were accompanied by their husbands and children. Most of her sister's children were now adults, with the exception of an eleven-year-old. He had his great grandfather's unruly ginger hair, and because of a birth injury, he limped. Eleanor's heart went out to him. She remembered how she had been the brunt of family jokes and cruel teasing at that age. She saved her best smile for him and invited him to join her at her table.

The boy's name was Julian. He had been born years after his siblings, and his mother had never really recovered from his birth. She had died when he was three, and her husband had been killed in a hunting accident several years later. He had been brought up by a governess and sent to boarding school at six. Eleanor thought about Lord Edward and how he, too, had been sent from home at an early age. Julian had been brought to the tea by his sister.

Twenty-Two

Chapter 22

J ulian.

Lady Eleanor had made discreet inquiries as to Julian's living arrangements. Most of the year, he was in school, but for holidays and for the summer, he was farmed out to different families. His only brother was in university and his sister had young children of her own to care for. The other family members were busy with their lives, and honestly, no one truly wanted to be responsible for an eleven-year-old boy. There wasn't a place for Julian anywhere.

While there was still no real friendship between the sisters, most had chosen to be civil. Those who appeared to cozy up to her were, for the most part, in need of a little monetary assistance. Eleanor would share her good fortune with them to a certain extent but had no need to buy their friendship.

Julian was different. Later, she would call them all to a family meeting, but first, she would see how Julian felt about a different arrangement.

Julian was on a school holiday, so he had been able to attend the family gathering. Eleanor approached his sister and asked if Julian would be allowed to visit her at her estate for the week. She would return him to his school at the proper time. His sister was only too happy to agree. Finding something for an eleven-year-old to do with three young children at home to care for was not easy.

When asked if he would like to visit this woman who was a stranger to him, Julian hesitated, but when he was told there would be dogs and horses at Eleanor's estate, he soon decided that might be more fun than doing nothing at his sister's house. His belongings were soon transferred to Eleanor's carriage. The gathering had come to a close, and after bidding everyone farewell, Eleanor and Julian left for her home.

Julian was quiet on the carriage ride. Eleanor tried to engage him in conversation, but the boy was shy and not used to being asked anything about himself. He always felt unwanted and had long practiced being invisible, but now this woman was addressing him personally. It was a new experience, and he wasn't sure he liked it.

Julian climbed down from the carriage slowly and carefully, favoring his bad leg, but when the dogs appeared, happy to see their mistress home, his face lit up with the only smile Eleanor had seen since meeting him. Pudgy and Penny were delighted to have a new admirer, and Julian was overjoyed. His first complete sentence since being introduced to Eleanor was to ask the dog's names and if he could play with them.

Eleanor had given him one of the guest bedrooms, but the

size of the house frightened him, so a small bed was placed in her dressing room, and the door to her bedroom was left open. Best of all, the dogs were happy to spend the night in his bed. Julian had never had a pet, and now two pups were cuddled up next to him.

He hadn't wanted to go to the tea. He hated it when the families got together. It reminded him that he was an orphan, but now he fell asleep with a smile on his face, thinking how lucky the day had turned out to be.

The next morning, breakfast was served on the terrace, and afterward, Eleanor took him to the stables to see the horses. Their size was overwhelming and frightened the young boy, but a pony that had once been used to pull a trap was perfect. Eleanor showed him how to hold a carrot in his hand and feed the animal.

Julian was soon busy brushing it, supervised by the stable master. The man was sure that there was a small saddle somewhere that would be a perfect fit for the pony. There was no reason that he couldn't be taught to ride. His leg would not be a problem. He would be an equal to anyone when on a horse. The boy fell asleep that night before his head hit the pillow. He couldn't remember ever having such a wonderful day.

The week had passed too quickly, and soon, it was time for Julian to return to school. As long as the talk was about the dogs or the pony, Julian was becoming quite the conversationalist, but if it was about anything else, he clammed up and became silent. Eleanor must broach the subject of his future before he returned to school and before she approached the family with the idea of becoming Julian's guardian.

A picnic basket had been prepared, and the two of them

walked down to the lake and spread a blanket. The dogs were happily chasing squirrels, much to the amusement of Eleanor and Julian, but now the time had come to discuss the future.

"You are to return to school tomorrow. The dogs and I shall miss you terribly, and I hope you will miss us. Would you like to come back to visit during your Christmas holiday? We would be delighted to have you. It could be arranged for you to live here with us if you would like to. You don't need to give me an answer now. Think about it, and we can talk about it at Christmas."

Julian stared at her. Eleanor was asking him if he wanted to return and spend Christmas at her house and if he would like to live with her permanently. He had never had a home of his own but had been passed from place to place as long as he could remember.

"Do you mean that I could live here always with the dogs and you?"

Eleanor had to laugh at the fact that the dogs had been his first choice. "Would that please you? I must speak with your aunts about it, but I don't think they would mind. If you decide after a year that you would be happy here, I could have a legal paper drawn up so that you and I would become a real family."

Julian turned away. Eleanor was afraid he was getting ready to say no, but then she realized he was trying to hide his tears. He had always felt unlovable, a nuisance that no one wanted. Could it be true? He had been trying not to like Eleanor, holding himself back, not daring to trust her, and yet now she was promising to give him a home and be his family. He had always dreamed of such a thing but never allowed himself to believe it could happen.

Twenty-Three

Chapter 23

Becoming a Family

Not only had Julian returned for the Christmas holidays, but after meeting with his brother and sister and all the aunts, it had been decided that if Eleanor wished to take on the responsibility of the eleven-year-old boy, they would have no objections. No longer would Julian be passed from house to house but would have a place to call his own.

He had his own room in his own home with someone who wanted him. It had taken him a while to feel safe and secure, but he had come to trust Eleanor, and when, a year later, he saw his name on the legal document that made him a part of her family forever, he knew it was real.

Mary Clair, too, had become part of his family. Being an astute observer of human nature, she had always worried about her sister-in-law's future. Eleanor's parents had never been lovable, and while she had cared a great deal for Lord Edward, she wasn't in love with him. Harold held a sexual attraction for her, but again, she wasn't in love.

Mary Clair had worried that when Eleanor did fall in love, it would be without restrictions. She would not only lose her heart but complete control over everything she owned. How dangerous that could be. As she watched Julian and Eleanor, she realized that time had come, but instead of it being a man who might break her heart and steal her money and property, it was this eleven year old boy. They had found each other, and the wounds that festered in each heart had been healed. They loved each other completely and unconditionally.

Epilogue

Only fairy tales end happily ever after....but because it is my tale to tell...that is how I will end it.

Lady Eleanor enjoyed her visits to Bath and amorous rendezvous with Harold and others for many years. She and Mary Clair took trips on the Orient Express and excursions to other far-off places. When he grew older, Julian would often accompany them on these adventures.

Mary Clair lived to a ripe old age, and her passing was peaceful. She left everything she owned to her godson, Julian.

Julian became an excellent horseman and a fine lawyer. He graduated from university with the highest of honors and later became a member of Parliament. In due time, he married, and Lady Eleanor became the happiest of grandmothers.

As the heir to the estates of Mary Clair and Lady Eleanor, he never needed to worry about money. He lived a long, rich, and happy life. His love for his aunt remained constant until her death.

About the Author

Elizabeth Moody is a pen name because I don't wish to shock some of my regular readers. Perhaps it will come as a surprise to some of my friends and family that I would write this book, but others think it is just another example of my active imagination and can't wait to read it.

Books by Julia Cammack

Bella, Book 1 "How to Play the Game of Life"

Bella, Book 2 "Winner Takes All"

Bridget, "A Journey from Rags to Riches"

2127jccam@gmail.com

www.ingramcontent.com/pod-product-compliance
Lightning Source LLC
Chambersburg PA
CBHW022036150726
47990CB00002B/992